Dazzling DIGGERS

For Kate, Tim, Henry and Angus – T.M.

KINGFISHER
An imprint of Kingfisher Publications Plc
New Penderel House, 283-288 High Holborn
London WC1V 7HZ

First published in hardback by Kingfisher 1997
First published in paperback by Kingfisher 1999
10 12 14 16 18 20 19 17 15 13 11

10TR/0704/TWP/FR/170ARM

Text copyright © Tony Mitton 1997
Illustrations copyright © Ant Parker 1997

A CIP catalogue record for this book is available from the British Library.

ISBN 0 7534 0350 1

Printed in Singapore

Dazzling DIGGERS

Tony Mitton and
Ant Parker

Lunch
box

KINGFISHER

Diggers are noisy, strong and big.

Diggers can carry and push and dig.

Diggers have shovels to scoop and lift,

blades that bulldoze, shunt and shift.

Diggers have buckets to gouge out ground,

breakers that crack and smash and pound.

Diggers move rubble and rocks and soil,

so diggers need drinks of diesel oil.

Some have tyres and some have tracks.

Some keep steady with legs called jacks.

Tyres and tracks grip hard as they travel,

squish through mud and grind through gravel.

Diggers go scrunch and squelch and slosh.

This dirty digger needs a hosepipe wash.

Diggers can bash and crash and break,

make things crumble, shiver and shake.

Diggers can heave and hoist and haul.

Diggers help buildings tower up tall.

Diggers park neatly, down on the site.

Then digger-drivers all go home. Goodnight.

Digger bits

levers

these control different parts of the digger

tyre

this helps the wheel to grip the ground and get the digger moving

bucket

this is for digging and scooping out

jack

this holds the digger steady when it is lifting or digging

piston

this is a strong pump that makes parts of the digger move about

breaker

this is for cracking concrete or lumps of rock

tracks

these help the digger to travel over slippery or bumpy ground

blade

this is for knocking down and pushing along